HAUNTED HOUSE

by Gill Davies
Illustrated by Eric Kincaid

Brimax · Newmarket · England

Haunted House

The Lonely House

Monty Mouse likes exploring. He loves to scamper along finding new places to run and skip. One day when Monty is playing hide and seek, he discovers an old, empty house on the edge of town. It is full of dust and cobwebs and seems lonely. Monty says, "You are a nice house. Please can I come in?"

Monty calls his brothers and sisters. "Come and look at my lovely Hideaway House."
The little mice run everywhere, peeping round doors and making the empty house echo to the sound of their happy voices. They like the pantry best. It is full of food - jars and bottles and cans and bags and packets.
"Yum! Yum!" says Sammy. "This place is great!"

9

"Why don't we come and live here?" suggests Sammy, munching a cookie.

"What a good idea," shouts Monty. "Let's go home and ask." Off rush the mice to tell Ma and Pa Whiskers all about the house.

"Hmm," says Pa. "It certainly sounds interesting. Your mother and I will take a look tomorrow." And so the next day they all go back to Hideaway House.

Ma and Pa Whiskers think
Hideaway House is wonderful.
"We will move here right away,"
they say. "Let us go home and
pack."
So the very next day the Whisker
family put all their belongings into
Pa's matchstick cart and move
into their new house.
As soon as they arrive, Monty
Mouse goes upstairs to explore.

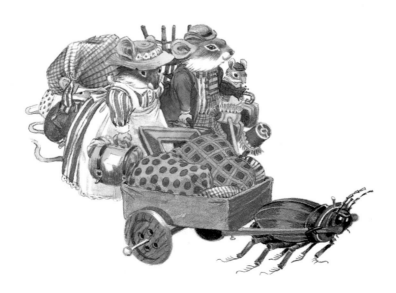

This is what Monty likes best. He runs everywhere, sniffing out every corner from the cool, dark cellar to the hot, dusty attic. Then he explores all the secret places in the tangled, overgrown garden. Monty is very happy. And so is Hideaway House. It is no longer sad and lonely. In fact, it is the happiest house in town.

Monty Mouse Meets Ghost

"I like night time in the garden," says Monty as he runs outside to smell the honeysuckle one warm summer night. Far away the town lights gleam and sparkle.

"Be careful that the owls don't eat you," calls Ma, but Monty is not afraid. He is friends with the owls, the bats, and the beetles.

Monty scampers a little way
along the path, and then
suddenly he sees a ghost!
A wavy, white shape rises out of
the undergrowth as Monty rubs
his eyes in amazement.
"Wooooooooo!" says the shape.
"Ooooooooeeer!" says Monty.
"Wooooooooo!" says the shape
again, moving up the path and
coming closer to Monty.

"Oooooeeer!" says Monty again, walking rapidly backwards.
"I am the Ghost of Hideaway House," announces the shape, pulling himself up tall. "Woooooo!" Monty stares up in astonishment.
"Wooo," wails Ghost again. "Why aren't you running away?"
"There is nowhere left to run," answers Monty, his back pressed against the wall.

"Anyway," says Monty, upset that his evening walk is being spoiled, "you should be haunting the house not the garden."
And then suddenly Ghost sinks down and begins to cry.
"I know," he sobs, "but the house is full of animals now. There's an owl in the haunted bedroom, and there's no room left for me."

Tears roll down Ghost's face.
"I think," says Monty, "that you
had better come inside."
"You poor dear!" says Ma, seeing
Ghost's sad face. "You look as if
you need some nice apple pie to
cheer you up."
Ghost smiles through his tears.
"I haven't eaten apple pie for a
long, long time – not once since
I have been dead," he says.

Ghost eats three fat slices of pie. It is delicious and he feels much better. Then Monty takes Ghost upstairs and shows him the spare bedroom on the top floor.
"This can be yours," he says.
Now Ghost is very happy. He has a lovely room with a view over the railway line, lots of new friends, and lots of apple pie.

The Rainy Day

Monty Mouse is bored. All his new friends are out or busy or asleep. He has been looking forward to making a den in the garden between the plant pots, but it is raining very hard and he cannot go outside.

The other mice play games, balancing on a cork, but Monty is too upset to join in.

"What about calling on Racer Rat?" suggests Ma Whiskers. "He might be lonely up there in the attic and would be glad to see you."

"What a good idea!" says Monty, cheering up. "I will do that right away." He scampers straight up the stairs. Half way up he meets Ghost.

"Can I come too?" asks Ghost.

"Of course," says Monty, and on they go together.

They soon reach the attic. Racer
Rat peeps out of a hole in the
ceiling and grins at his friends.
"Hi there! Come on up," he cries.
"It's nice of you to come and visit
on such a rainy day."
The rain is pounding loudly on
the attic roof as Ghost, carrying
Monty, oozes up the ladder and
through the hole.

The attic is a lovely, jumbly sort of place that is full of boxes and books and pictures.

Legs the Spider sits on the edge of the skylight. He watches the world outside and the rain pouring down as the friends talk and laugh.

"Hey, everyone!" shouts Legs all of a sudden. "The rain has stopped."

"At last!" say Racer and Monty Mouse and Ghost all together. "Yippee!" shouts Monty. "Now I can make my den."
They all say good-bye. Then Ghost and Monty fly downstairs. Monty has a lovely afternoon. He makes a great den between the flower pots. But every now and then he stops to wave to Legs and Racer who are watching him from the high attic window.

Ma has a Shock!

It is snowing.
When Monty Mouse wakes up,
he is very excited to see that the
world outside is all white.
As soon as they are dressed, all
the mice children rush outside to
play. They throw snowballs and
slide and build a snow mouse
while Pa clears a path.
Suddenly they hear Ma scream.

"Whatever is the matter?" cries Pa, rushing inside without taking off his boots.

There in the porch is Jim Fox, the tramp. He is fast asleep and snoring loudly. Ma Whiskers is terrified and is shaking all over. All the animals from Hideaway House look nervously around the door.

"If I know Jim Fox, he'll stay until Spring now," says Frog.

"Oh no!" cries Ma Whiskers starting to shake again. "He can't! He just can't!"

Pa takes her out into the dining room, and all the animals tiptoe after them.

Meanwhile Ghost comes down to find out what is happening. He has heard Ma screaming.

Ghost hopes Ma is all right. He has grown very fond of Ma Whiskers – and her apple pie. "What is the matter?" he asks. Monty explains and then adds, "Foxes always mean trouble and Ma's terrified of them."

"I know!" says Ghost. "Why don't I haunt Jim Fox and see if I can frighten him away."

"What a great idea!" says Monty.

"Please help me," begs Ma Whiskers as Jim Fox sneezes, yawns and sits up to scratch. Ghost practices swooshing and whoooing a few times. This is a difficult task for Ghost since his white shape disappears in the snow and the wind is howling louder than Ghost can. Finally Ghost is ready, but when he goes out on the porch, he finds that Jim Fox has gone back to sleep.

At last Ghost makes a fine, wailing whoosh at Jim, and sends his torn old hat flying into the snowy sky. Startled awake, Jim Fox jumps up and chases his hat down the street. He decides to find a more peaceful place to stay.

Ma Whiskers is delighted. She gives Ghost a whole apple pie just for him. He grins, saying between bites, "That was fun. I haven't had a good haunt for ages."

Silk Wood

Fluffytuft has an Idea

"Nothing is nicer to wake up to than a Spring morning in Silk Wood," says Mrs Squirrel.
She tickles Fluffytuft's nose with her feather duster, but he pretends to be asleep and pulls the covers up over his nose.
"Stop it! Go away! I'm still asleep!" he squeals, rolling into a ball as the duster whisks around his toes.

"You won't want any breakfast then," says Mrs Squirrel. "Young squirrels who are fast asleep find it difficult to eat hot toast and peanut butter."
Fluffytuft thinks about breakfast and finally tumbles out of bed. He pulls on his dungarees and then settles down to enjoy slice after slice of toast.

"Today," announces Fluffytuft,
"I am going to lay an egg."
"Don't be silly," says Mrs Squirrel.
"Birds and snakes and butterflies
lay eggs – not squirrels."
"I don't care!" says Fluffytuft,
putting his plate into the sink. "It
is Spring. All the birds have eggs
in their nests. They have been
singing about it every day. Why
should they have all the fun?"

Rosie Rabbit is waiting outside to play with Fluffytuft.

"Hi, Rosie," says Fluffytuft. "Today I am going to lay an egg."

"Lay an egg!" laughs Rosie. "You are silly, Fluffytuft. Squirrels don't lay eggs!"

And she laughs so much she has to sit down and dab the tears away with her handkerchief.

"You are very rude to laugh at me," says Fluffytuft, feeling cross.

Fluffytuft marches off down the woodland path.

It is a wonderful day and soon Fluffytuft forgets to be cross. The sun beams down and the bluebells smell wonderful. The birds are singing, their nests snug full of eggs. Soon Fluffytuft too will lay an egg. He is sure of that.

"I am off to find my very own egg," he tells everyone he meets.

Fluffytuft Lays an Egg

Fluffytuft sits by the waterfall and watches the bubbles dance.
"I like waterfalls," he says to Kingfisher. "They make such a nice rushing-gushing sound."
"Hmmm ..." mutters Kingfisher, dreaming of silvery fish to eat.
Rosie Rabbit comes skipping over the bridge to join Fluffytuft.

"Hi, Fluffytuft," calls Rosie. "Have you found an egg to hatch yet?" She giggles and Fluffytuft frowns. "Stop it, Rosie!" he says. "Don't you dare laugh at me again." He stands up, shaking his tail angrily. Then Fluffytuft sets off again along the bank. He is running so quickly he does not see the twisted tree roots on the bank and catches his toes on them.

Yow! Bump! Splash! Fluffytuft
tumbles down into a pool.
"Oh dear!" he groans. "I am
completely wet through and
covered in mud."
And then he sees the egg. It is
resting in a hollow. It is smooth,
shiny, and white with speckles.
No-one is sitting on it.
"Hello, little egg," says Fluffytuft.
"Would you like to belong to me?
I can take good care of you."

Fluffytuft is so excited to find an egg of his very own that he does not realise it is not an egg at all. It is a pebble – a beautiful egg-shaped pebble.
Fluffytuft builds a mound of grass and moss and then lays the egg carefully on top.
"There," he says. "Now I have laid an egg."
Fluffytuft sits on his nest all afternoon and waits for his egg to hatch. But nothing happens.

At last Fluffytuft jumps off the nest and peers inside. But his egg has disappeared. Has it hatched already and run away? Big tears are rolling down Fluffytuft's face when Rosie Rabbit arrives and asks, "Why are you crying?"

"I found my egg and then I hatched it, but now it has run away!" sobs Fluffytuft.

Rosie plunges her paws deep into the nest and pulls out his egg.

"Oh, Fluffytuft," she laughs. "Your egg is a pebble. It is so heavy it has fallen to the bottom."

Now Fluffytuft laughs too. "What a silly squirrel I am!" he squeals, rolling on the ground.

The friends paint the pebble and give it to Mrs Squirrel. She says, "You know, if it wasn't for these patterns, you might think this was an egg. Now why are you two giggling?"

Fluffytuft's Wonderful Tail

Fluffytuft has a wonderful tail. It is bushy and red, and he is very proud of it. But he cannot see it easily. When Fluffytuft twists around his tail always whisks out of view. Trying to look at it in the mirror, Fluffytuft bounces up and down on the bed. But still he can catch only a glimpse as his handsome tail flashes past.

One lovely summer afternoon Fluffytuft goes to the Silver Pool at the edge of Silk Wood.

"Now," he says, "I shall be able to see my tail properly. It will be reflected in the shining lake if I stand in the right place."

"Where is the best spot to get a good view of my tail?" Fluffytuft asks Glurk the Frog, who is sitting on a lily pad. Glurk croaks and sings his answer:

"Over Buttercup Meadow,
Beyond the willow tree
Where the sun slants down
And the breeze flies free."
Glurk is right. The water makes
a perfect mirror there. Fluffytuft
stares into the water and can
see a handsome, fluffy, red tail.
"Wow!" he says. "Is that
wonderful tail really mine?"
"Certainly not!" a voice answers,
"It is mine!"

There, smiling at him, is a cheeky, little fox cub called Frisky.

"That tail in the water is definitely mine," says Fluffytuft.

"Since you seem so friendly, I do not like to argue the minute we meet," says Frisky. "But I assure you that tail is mine."

Glurk says, "You are both wrong. Since you are standing close together, it looks like one tail. Move apart."

Frisky and Fluffytuft step apart; and there, reflected in the Silver Pool, are two adorable, fluffy, red tails. The new friends play happily together all afternoon and compare their handsome, red tails as Glurk paints pictures of them. Now Fluffytuft has a portrait to hang on the wall. He no longer needs to bounce up and down in front of the mirror to see his wonderful tail.

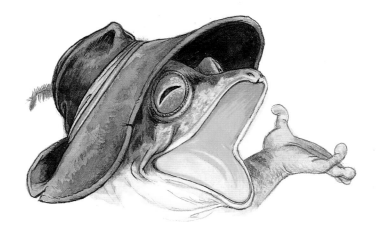

The Surprise Party

Fluffytuft wakes up feeling excited. Today is Old Man Otter's birthday. The woodland folk are very fond of the lovely, kind, old otter and plan a surprise party that night.

Mrs Squirrel is baking a birthday cake. Mr Squirrel is making a new deckchair for Old Man Otter. Fluffytuft says: "I want to make him a present too."

"Why don't you lay him an egg?" says Mr Squirrel, laughing. Then Mrs Squirrel makes some suggestions. "You could paint a nice picture." "No," says Fluffytuft, "that is silly." "Why not make a calendar?" "That," says Fluffytuft, "is boring." "What about a newspaper hat?" "No," says Fluffytuft. "You have some really stupid ideas." "Don't be rude!" says Mrs Squirrel, going into the pantry for flour.

Feeling cross, Fluffytuft goes out for a walk. He meets Rosie Rabbit.

"What are you giving Old Man Otter for his birthday?" he asks.

"I don't know," says Rosie.

"Neither do I," says Fluffytuft, glad that he is not the only one who doesn't know. The two friends sit down to think, but they still have no ideas. Suddenly Frisky comes running along the path.

"Glurk the Frog has written a song about Old Man Otter," says Frisky. "He wants us to sing it at the birthday party tonight."
Frisky, Rosie and Fluffytuft practise the song all day. At last it is night. Swans glide over the Silver Pool with streamers and balloons, and woodland folk carry lanterns as they gather around the lake's edge. Old Man Otter wakes up. He is amazed to see so many friends clapping and cheering for him.

Old Man Otter is thrilled with his presents and birthday cake, but he loves the song best of all. Glurk plays his violin as Fluffytuft, Rosie and Frisky sing sweetly;

"We love you so much, and we all agree, you're the dearest old man in the world, you see."

"This is the loveliest present of all," says Old Man Otter, tears running down his whiskered nose.

Then they all dance until dawn.

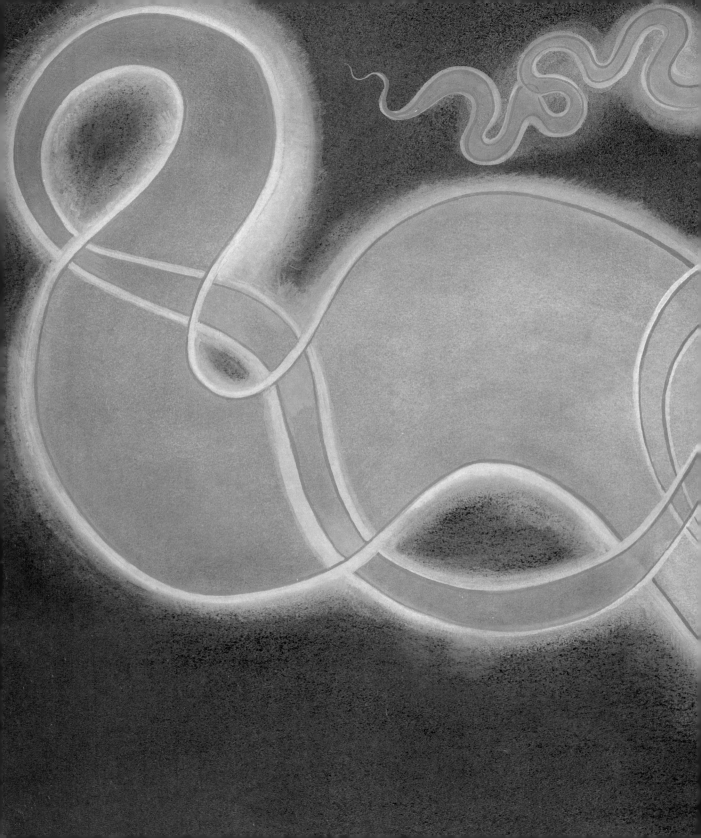